How Tevye
Became a Milkman

How Tevye
Became a Milkman
by Gabriel Lisowski

Holt, Rinehart and Winston · New York

Copyright © 1976 by Gabriel Lisowski
Adapted by permission of the Family of Sholem Aleichem
from a story by Sholem Aleichem.
All rights reserved, including the right to reproduce
this book or portions thereof in any form.
Published simultaneously in Canada by Holt, Rinehart
and Winston of Canada, Limited.
Printed in the United States of America
10 9 8 7 6 5 4   3 2 1
Library of Congress Cataloging in Publication Data
Lisowski, Gabriel.
    How Tevye became a milkman.
    SUMMARY: A poor peasant is richly rewarded for
helping two ladies find their way home from the forest.
    1. Rabinowitz, Shalom, 1859-1916. Dos groyse
gevins. English. II. Title.
PZ7.L6915Ho   [Fic]   76-8226
ISBN 0-03-016636-5

To Fania

In a small village in the Ukraine
stood an old wooden house,
with a dilapidated barn leaning
against it. Tevye, his wife and their
seven daughters lived here.
They were very poor.

Tevye chopped and hauled wood.

Fastnik, his horse, pulled the cart from the forest
to the railroad station.
That's how Tevye earned a living.
Even when he worked, he hardly earned enough
to feed his family.

"We starve three times a day,"
he often said, "at breakfast, lunch
and again at suppertime."

One summer evening as Tevye and Fastnik
were on their way home from the railroad station,
a wheel fell off the cart.
Tevye jumped down to fix it.
It was growing dark when he started for home again.

The shapes and shadows in
the forest made Tevye nervous.
However much
he snapped the reins,
Fastnik took his sweet time,
crawling along.

Then a branch got caught in a wheel
and the cart ground to a halt.
Cursing his luck, Tevye again jumped down.
No sooner had he removed the branch,
when an owl hooted overhead,
frightening Fastnik and sending him
galloping away.

Tevye ran after him and caught him.
He said a few harsh words to the horse,
then climbed back up and continued on his way.
By now, it was so dark,
Tevye was sure he saw robbers and devils
behind every bush.
To pretend to himself that he wasn't frightened,
he began to sing at the top of his lungs:

Giddy-ap you dope,
It's getting dark.
Oy vay!
You're a horse
Like I'm a hero
Giddy-ap Hey! Hey!

Suddenly he heard some cries from behind.
"Help! Please Help!"

Tevye pretended he hadn't heard and rode on.
"Help! Please help!" the voices cried again.
"Probably robbers or devils trying to deceive me,"
he said. Although Tevye was eager to keep going,
something made him stop.

He rode back a short way
and found two frightened women.
"My mother-in-law and I were out walking
and we got lost," said the younger woman.
"Please take us home."
Tevye looked them over,
wondering if they were trying to trick him.
"Where is your home?" he asked, suspiciously.
"We live in the green house,
at the edge of the forest," said the young woman.
Tevye whistled. The green house!
The richest family in town lived there.

Tevye got down and helped the women into the cart.
He hummed to himself as they jogged along.
Soon they saw the lights of the green house
shining through the trees.
As the cart entered the courtyard,
a young man rushed out.
"Wife! Mother!" he cried. He turned to Tevye.
"Thank you for bringing them home," he said.
"I was sick with worry. Come! Let us celebrate."

Tables were heaped with plates of boiled chicken,
roast turkey, fish and meats of all kinds,
cookies and cakes and whatnot and everyone
sat down to eat.
The young man asked Tevye about his family.
Tevye told them about his life of poverty.

"We will help you!" the young man cried.
He put baskets on the table
and everybody put money and food into them.
Then he said, "We have a cow
which is not too beautiful, but she gives milk.
You can have her too."

Tevye sang all the way home.

His wife, hearing his voice,
came rushing out to meet him.
Tevye told her what happened.
She clapped her hands in delight.
With milk, butter and cheese
to have and to sell,
they would never be hungry again.
Tevye and his wife called
to their seven daughters
and they all danced and cried
and were happy.

And that is how Tevye, once a hauler of timber, became a milkman.